RALPH *and the* QUEEN'S BATHTUB

By Kay Chorao

The Repair of Uncle Toe

Ralph and the Queen's Bathtub

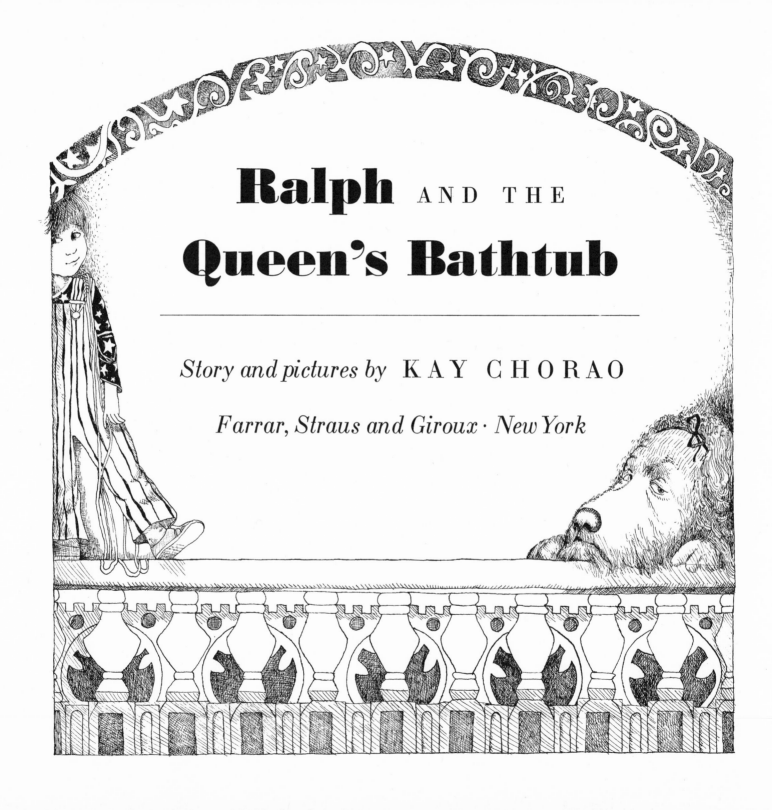

Ralph AND THE Queen's Bathtub

Story and pictures by KAY CHORAO

Farrar, Straus and Giroux · New York

For Peter

RALPH *and the* QUEEN'S BATHTUB

ALPH could walk to school alone now. Everyone said it was fine to be *that* old.

But Ralph wondered.

Sometimes he walked with his older brother, Nicky. But usually Nicky ran ahead, leaving Ralph all alone except for Elda, who didn't count.

She wore a sign that read:

> *I'm Elda.*
> *I belong to Miss Liverstay's kindergarten.*
> *Please take me to room 102 if I get lost.*

No matter who Ralph walked with, though, he passed the Queen's Bathtub, a scaly tall house, haunted by a giant witch. Sometimes Ralph saw her face at the window, ugly as a meat grinder. And once he saw hands, like giant claws, reach for a bag of groceries delivered to the side door.

Ralph's earliest memories were of being spanked for licking mothballs, and of seeing that witch at her window.

Ralph was still in a stroller the first time he saw her. Nicky had whispered, "She eats little children." And Ralph never forgot it.

Even now when he walked by the Queen's Bathtub on the way to school, he thought to himself, "She eats little children." He shivered and wondered if she had rows of teeth for shredding up little boys.

(Sometimes Ralph even let Elda catch up with him, so he wouldn't be quite alone.)

After school, Ralph usually went to the park with his mother and his little brother, Claude, who was two and a half.

"Park now, Mom," Claude would yell when he heard Ralph come in.

"Don't yell like you're ordering a plate of spaghetti," Ralph would grumble.

But Claude would grin and give Ralph a hug.

Then they would gather pails and shovels and dump trucks.

Ralph would find his rope, which was gray and lumpy with knots. It sat next to his football, which was shiny new, like a big brown egg.

"That's baby junk, going to the playground," Rinaldo and Arty
said, when Ralph passed them.

Ralph pretended not to hear.

But as soon as they got to the park, Ralph ran away by himself
and roped a tree and climbed into the branches where no one could
see how wet his eyes were. He liked the park. He could practice
roping and climbing and he didn't have to talk to anyone. And if
he made a mistake, no one made fun.

His mother said he was a monkey.

Ralph said he was Tarzan.

When he felt like it, Ralph went to the sandbox.

The little children treated him like a visiting king. They stared at him and admired his mud pies.

"Yum-yum," said Ralph, pretending to eat a mud pie.

"Yum-yum," echoed Claude, jamming a fist full of sand into his mouth.

Then Claude's face wrinkled up at the terrible taste and Ralph had to rush him into a swing and push him high so he would forget to howl.

Ralph squinted at the funny shapes of light coming through the leaves overhead.

"Kick the stars, Claudie, and the eyeballs and the fish and the witch teeth."

No one knew what on earth Ralph was talking about except Ralph himself.

But Claude smiled, as if he understood, too.

One day just as they were leaving for the park, Ralph's father came home from work a little early.

"Aren't you getting too old to hang around the playground?" he said.

Ralph looked at his feet.

"Why don't you play with some boys your own age?"

"Rinaldo and Arty always play war. And I hate playing war," said Ralph.

"Then play with Nicky and *his* friends," said his father.

"Nicky said that if I show my face at his secret club, Bo-bo will cream me," said Ralph.

"Nonsense," said Ralph's father.

Ralph looked at his mother for help. But his mother looked at his father.

"Come along on the elevator. Nicky is down in the basement

somewhere," she said.

So Ralph went to the basement alone. He could hear Claude

up on the first floor. "Ralph with ME," howled Claude. He howled

all the way out the front door until his voice faded away.

Ralph opened a pack of Black Cat gum and put two sticks in his mouth. He did it one stick at a time to make the job last. Then he examined the walls and floors for roaches and water bugs. There were five cockroaches and one water bug, who ambled under an old light plug.

"It's your brother spying around," said a voice.

The voice belonged to Bo-bo Berger. He was president of Nicky's club.

"This place is private," said Bo-bo, opening a door.

Ralph couldn't think of a thing to say. He just looked into the broom closet where Bo-bo and Nicky and some others sat. So that was the secret club! It smelled of floor mops.

"I suppose you've come down here to spy," said a boy with a spoon stuck behind his ear.

Ralph still couldn't think of a thing to say.

"Buzz off," said Bo-bo.

"Maybe you had better go to the park with Mom," said Nicky.

"He's hanging around for some lemonade," said the spoon boy, stirring some lemonade the color of asparagus.

"Go play on the seesaws," said Bo-bo.

"And the swings," said the lemonade boy.

"And the sandbox," said a boy with a plastic bow tie.

Then they all laughed and pointed at Ralph.

Ralph still couldn't think of a thing to say. But he stared at the pitcher and *spat*. His gum flew through the air and landed with a plop right in the middle of the asparagus-green lemonade.

"Contamination!" yelled Bo-bo.

Ralph didn't wait to hear more. He ran. He ran up the steps, through the lobby, and out the front door. He ran out to the sidewalk and up the block.

He wanted to run to the park. He wanted to bury his head in his mother's lap and say those boys were mean. But he didn't go to the park. His mother had sent him away. She didn't want him.

He wanted to run home and hide in his room. But his father would say, "Why aren't you out playing with the boys? And that football I bought you is just sitting in your room."

So Ralph ran. He ran toward school, crossing the only streets he was allowed to cross, the only streets he knew.

He ran until he reached a door, tall and black as licorice. There were tiny windows like gumdrops all around the door. He wanted to peep. No one had ever peeped inside. Maybe it was called the Queen's Bathtub because there was a huge bathtub inside. Maybe the giant took baths there. All the time. Without clothes. Maybe.

Ralph peeked.

But before he knew what was happening, a hand snatched him into the house.

"Why are you snooping around?" said the giant.

Ralph wanted to plug his ears because her voice hurt. He wanted to say, "You smell funny, let me go." But his voice wouldn't work.

"WELL?" said the giant.

Ralph felt he might cry.

"I don't taste good," he said.

"And who does?" said the giant.

Her face was pasty white. Maybe she lived on horse glue, children, and white bread.

"A kid named Elda. She's fat and juicy," said Ralph.

"I'm not interested. I don't like kids. Not to look at. Not to listen to. Not to *eat*," snapped the giant.

"Me neither," said Ralph.

"Then why are you snooping around?" she said.

Ralph shrugged his shoulders. How could he tell her? About the bathtub, and wanting to see *her*?

He peeped into the living room.

Instead of a bathtub, there was a sofa shaped like sausage. A dog the color of potatoes lay on it.

"That's Sylvia," said the giant. "Don't get ideas of patting him. He doesn't like boys any better than I do."

Sylvia looked at Ralph and scratched a flea.

"Sylvia's a girl's name," said Ralph.

"He doesn't know that, and don't tell him," snapped the giant.

"Are you a witch?" said Ralph.

"Not only a witch but a vampire, a wolf-woman, a crocodile monster, a bride of Wolf-man, and a vegetable Thing, among others."

The giant pointed to the posters all over the walls.

"Are those *you*?" said Ralph.

"Of course they're me. I was a movie star," said the giant, patting the nest of ringlets that quivered around on her head like a platter of junket.

"I never met a movie star," said Ralph. He wondered if movie stars all had that odd musty smell and lived in houses with the shades pulled down like eyelids half shut.

"Is that why you came? You came in here to fool me, to trick me into showing some of my old movies? The neighbor people must have told you. They spy, you know." The giant narrowed her eyes at Ralph.

"I didn't know," said Ralph. He knew his eyes were getting wet. If only she wouldn't *stare* at him with her yellow eyes half shut like the window shades. If only she would say, "This is a bad dream. Now wake up and I will give you a lollipop."

But she didn't say that. She said, "My name's Dolly Mitten. And don't snivel."

Ralph wiped his nose. "I want to go now," he said.

"Where? Up? Down? Or sideways?" cackled Dolly Mitten.

"Out," said Ralph, putting his weight against a door and wiggling the knob. The door flew open and Ralph fell into a dining room.

"That's private!" Dolly yelled.

"That's a mess," said Ralph.

Everything was covered with dust. And in the dust were
pictures, drawn with a line as broad as Dolly's finger.

"Don't spy on my dust drawings," said Dolly, jutting her lower lip.

"That's neat," said Ralph. "I wish our house could get as dirty as that." He made a thing the shape of a cough drop. "That's a football. I hate it. Once I slipped on a Tootsie wrapper trying to catch it. I got hurt and Rinaldo and Arty laughed their heads off."

"Things thrown by boys are always nasty," said Dolly. "When I was still a movie star, boys threw awful things at me. All the time. Eggs, sticks, bottles, stones, mushy tomatoes . . ."

Ralph grinned.

"It's not funny. Those boys drove me into this house where I've stayed ever since."

"I'm not laughing at that. It's just that I never met anyone who hated footballs before. I thought I was the only one," said Ralph.

Dolly pursed her lips like two wrinkled oven mits.

"You still want to go?" she said.

"Yes."

"Then try going UP," she shouted. Then she cackled and scooped Ralph up and put him inside a dumbwaiter.

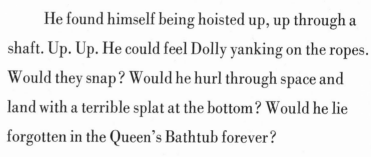
He found himself being hoisted up, up through a shaft. Up. Up. He could feel Dolly yanking on the ropes. Would they snap? Would he hurl through space and land with a terrible splat at the bottom? Would he lie forgotten in the Queen's Bathtub forever?

But the yanking stopped. The platform stopped.

"Push open the door," yelled Dolly.

Ralph pushed a square door in front of him, and stepped into a solarium as big as a cornfield. It was stuffed with growing things.

Dolly's head appeared over a staircase.

"You like my garden? Vegetables, you know. Corn, carrots, lettuce, turnips, parsnips . . ."

Ralph nodded. "You have a back yard upstairs," he said.

"You tickle my funny bone," said the giant.

She smiled, but Ralph didn't smile back. He felt like Claude's teddy bear, the one Claude hugged and played with but would toss on the floor when he was in a temper. The teddy bear had a music box in its stomach, but now the music box was just a square lump without a key. Because Claude had smashed it.

Ralph held his stomach. "I want to go home," he whispered.

Sylvia lumbered up the stairs. Ralph couldn't run down that way.

"Since you are such a jolly little turnip, would you like to see one of my movies?" said Dolly.

Her eyes gleamed yellow. Ralph was afraid to say no. Maybe she would pick him up and smash him.

So he didn't say anything, not even when Dolly picked him up and slapped him onto her back like a knapsack.

She carried him up some steps to a room lined with rubber masks. The masks had empty eye holes.

"We will have such fancy times," said Dolly.

Ralph didn't say anything.

Dolly turned on a movie projector. Then she sat in a chair as big as a throne.

Sylvia lay at the top of the stairs, so Ralph couldn't run down.

"Dancing the Moonlight Willies," said the movie title.

But Ralph scarcely saw it. How would he get out? Would he be trapped in the Queen's Bathtub forever? Would he have to live on Dolly's vegetables and never eat another Popsicle again? Would his mother cry? Would his father cry, too, into a large white handkerchief with his head bent down so that everyone would think that he was really just blowing his nose?

There was Dolly on the screen, tall as a moose, and wearing a floppy white dress. Her face had stitches. The real Dolly was crumpled up on her throne, enjoying what she saw.

"Sylvia needs his ears scratched," Ralph said.

"Yes, it is a good scene, isn't it?" Dolly said.

"No. I said Sylvia needs his ears scratched," yelled Ralph.

"Hush, boy. Come here, Sylvia," Dolly said crossly.

Sylvia lumbered over and sat on Dolly's feet.

This was Ralph's chance.

Taking a quick glance back, he shot down the stairs two at a
time. The image of Dolly standing there screaming at him was locked
in Ralph's memory. Even in that glance, he saw the movie picture of
Dolly projected all over the real Dolly as she stood there yelling.

"Come back, you silly turnip. Don't run away," yelled Dolly.

But Ralph didn't stop. He heard footsteps slamming down after him, but he ran and ran without stopping.

He reached the licorice door. It was *stuck*. He pulled and wobbled the knob. It wouldn't budge. He could hear Dolly coming down the second staircase. The bolt. He forgot the bolt. But she was coming. His fingers fumbled as he pushed the bolt, but then it slid open with a thump. Dolly was coming. He could feel her near him.

With all the strength he could muster, he pulled the front knob and the door flew open. He felt the brush of Sylvia's fur on his leg as he ran out.

OUT! He was out of the Queen's Bathtub!

Ralph didn't stop running until he reached his own building.

He was still breathless when his father opened the apartment door.

"Ralph, where have you been?" said his father.

"Ralph, we've been so worried," said his mother.

"Hey, that was neat when you spit your gum in the lemonade," said Nicky.

Claude didn't say anything. He just hugged Ralph.

"I went to a terrible place. There was a giant witch and dust and a vegetable garden upstairs and a masky room up higher," said Ralph.

"You're talking gibberish," said Ralph's father.

"Your imagination is running away with you," said Ralph's mother.

Tears were coming down Ralph's cheeks, so his mother washed them away with a cloth that was a little too cold, the way it was always a little too cold. And his father smoothed his hair the way he always smoothed his hair. And Ralph felt better.

Then Ralph's mother sniffed the air and ran to the kitchen.

"I burned the peas again," she said.

Ralph smiled, because his mother always burned the peas. And he was glad to be home.

That night, Ralph lay in his bottom bunk staring at Nicky's bedsprings.

"Tomorrow those guys are going to get you for spitting in the lemonade," said Nicky.

"I don't care," said Ralph. He *did* care, but after all, he had outsmarted a giant.

"Want to toss the football around tomorrow?" said Nicky.

"One of these days I will. But tomorrow I'm going to teach Rinaldo and Arty how to rope and climb," said Ralph.

Then he closed his eyes and dreamed of giant footballs shrinking and shrinking into tiny green things that burned in the bottom of his mother's pot.